Dedicated to Andy, who is working on
making his own wishes come true

First published in the United States of America in April 2012
by Walker Publishing Company, Inc., a division of Bloomsbury Publishing, Inc.
www.bloomsburykids.com

For information about permission to reproduce selections from this book, write to
Permissions, Walker BFYR, 175 Fifth Avenue, New York, New York 10010

Library of Congress Cataloging-in-Publication Data
Richards, Chuck.
Lulu's magic wand / Chuck Richards.
p.      cm.
Summary: While on a family trip to Adventure Planet amusement park, young Lulu accidentally gets a real magic wand
as a prize and her wishes magically begin to come true, placing her family and other visitors in terrible danger.
ISBN 978-0-8027-2248-5 (hardcover)  •  ISBN 978-0-8027-2249-2 (reinforced)
[1. Magic—Fiction. 2. Amusement parks—Fiction. 3. Imagination—Fiction.] I. Title.
PZ7.R37858Lul 2012          [E]—dc23          2011025719

Art created with colored pencil and acrylic on paper
Typeset in Hadriano Std Light
Book design by Regina Roff

Printed in China by C&C Offset Printing Co., Ltd., Shenzhen, Guangdong
2  4  6  8  10  9  7  5  3  1  (hardcover)
2  4  6  8  10  9  7  5  3  1  (reinforced)

The Winklewigs had planned all winter long for their family trip to Adventure Planet. The long wait was finally over. Today would be a wish come true for little Lulu Winklewig.

"Look, Sally. It's the Wizardly World of Wonder!" announced Junior. "Let's give it a shot, Dad."

Lulu spotted her favorite picture-book character—Priscilla, the Fairy Piglet—among all the game prizes. She wanted her dad to win that plump pink pig!

Junior took aim and hit the bull's-eye on his very first turn. He chose a goofy dragon hat for his trophy. But when Dad tried to win a prize for Lulu, his pitches all missed the target.

Dad and Junior took three more turns, but Lulu had to be happy with a small prize. She chose a magic wand that looked just like Priscilla's, with a star that seemed to glow and sparkle.

Lulu really wanted to ride the merry-go-round, so she and Dad got in line.
While they waited, Lulu watched a clown make balloon animals.

As she imagined all the balloon critters running wild and free, Lulu wished a
wish and waved her wand.

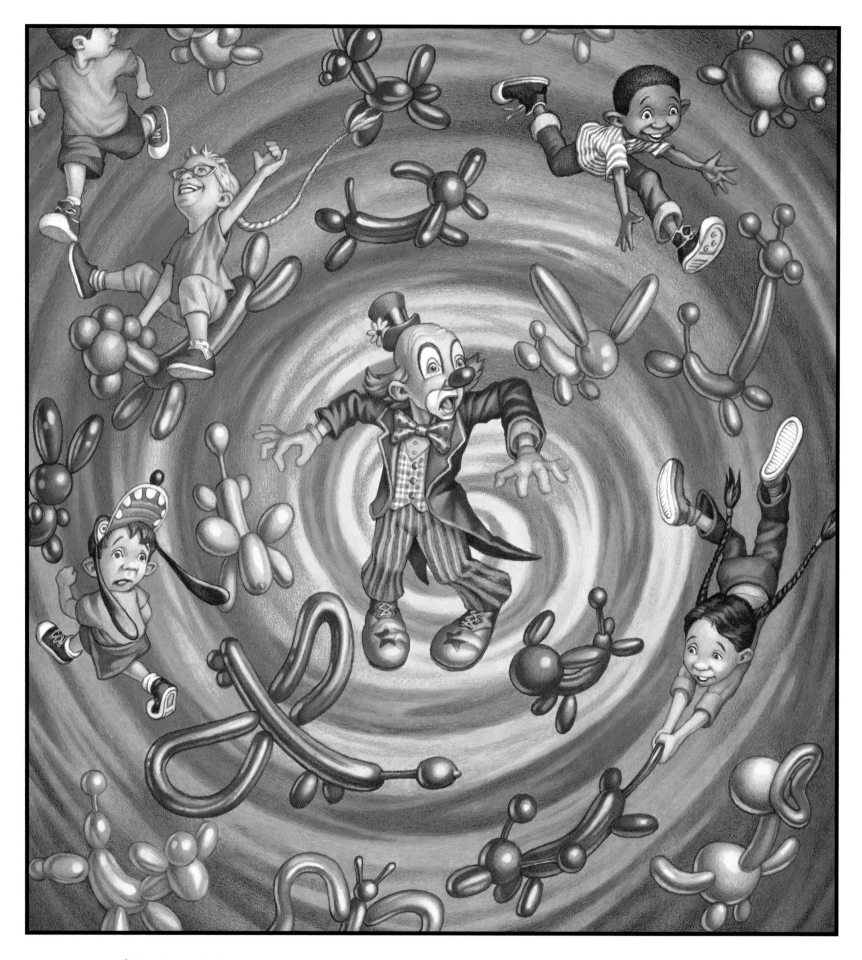

All of a sudden, the balloons swirled around and around as children scrambled to catch them. Dad thought that the balloons had simply been stirred up by a gust of wind.

After they climbed aboard the carousel, Dad planted Lulu on top of a gigantic queen bee. He jumped on a well-dressed bullfrog just as the merry-go-round began to move.

As Lulu circled around and around, she wondered what it would be like to fly like a bee over Adventure Planet. She raised her hand and waved the wand again. The bee instantly took flight along with all the other merry-go-round creatures!

"Look at me go!" cried Lulu.

Everyone on the ground looked like tiny little ants as Lulu and the bee zoomed higher and higher.

Dad's bullfrog landed on the track of the Screamin' Dragon roller coaster just as it pulled off the ground and slithered through the park like a gigantic iron snake.

"Run for cover!" shrieked Dad.

The dragon blazed around the loop-de-loop, then shot straight toward him. Dad's pudgy toad sprang out of the speeding serpent's path, only a split second away from becoming roadkill.

An eerie, high-pitched whirring noise echoed through the park, and everyone
looked up toward the sky. Flying saucers had arrived from Milky Way City!

The Martian star fleet circled the Octo-Beast, then used laser beams to make her spin faster and faster—until she lifted off the ground like a mother ship.

Back at the arcade, the wizard had turned the Wizardly World of Wonder upside down searching for his *real* magic wand. He tried wand after wand, but none of them worked.

Meanwhile, Lulu sailed high above the amusement park. She felt just like Priscilla, the Fairy Piglet—she could wish for anything that popped into her pretty pigtailed head.

Without warning, the Raging Jungle Rapids roared through the arcade. The wizard was swept away by the floodwaters, but managed to stay afloat by grabbing hold of a passing piglet.

Suddenly the wizard remembered the little girl who had wanted the fairy pig but had to settle for a magic wand earlier that day. Now he knew how to get to the bottom of this hocus-pocus.

Back in the Wilderness Outpost, a towering tyrannosaurus was hunting for breakfast. A posse of cowboys was trying to round up the rampaging skeleton with their lassos.

"You kids go find Lulu!" screamed Mom as the dinosaur closed in on her.
Sally and Junior escaped, but the bony beast cornered Mom and the buckaroos,
gulping them down one by one into his rib-cage jail.

Oscar, the park mascot, had left the entrance gate when Dad's bullfrog landed on his tasseled hat.

The long-legged monkey plucked Dad off his frog and stuffed him snugly between his lips. Then Oscar climbed to the top of the wiggly roller coaster and gleefully swung back and forth, hanging by his tail.

Meanwhile, Junior and Sally raced around a corner and were nearly mowed down by the waterlogged wizard. He grabbed Junior by the collar.

"Your little sister's got my wand! Just take a look around . . . a magic wand is no toy for a toddler!"

The three of them piled onto a flying cow and took off to look for Lulu.

Flying above the chaos, Sally thought she heard a familiar voice call for help.
It was her dad, sinking slowly into Oscar's goofy grin!
"Stop that monkey!" shouted Sally.

Junior steered the cow to chase the mascot, but they couldn't put an end to his monkey business.

Lulu heard the yelling and flew over for a closer look.

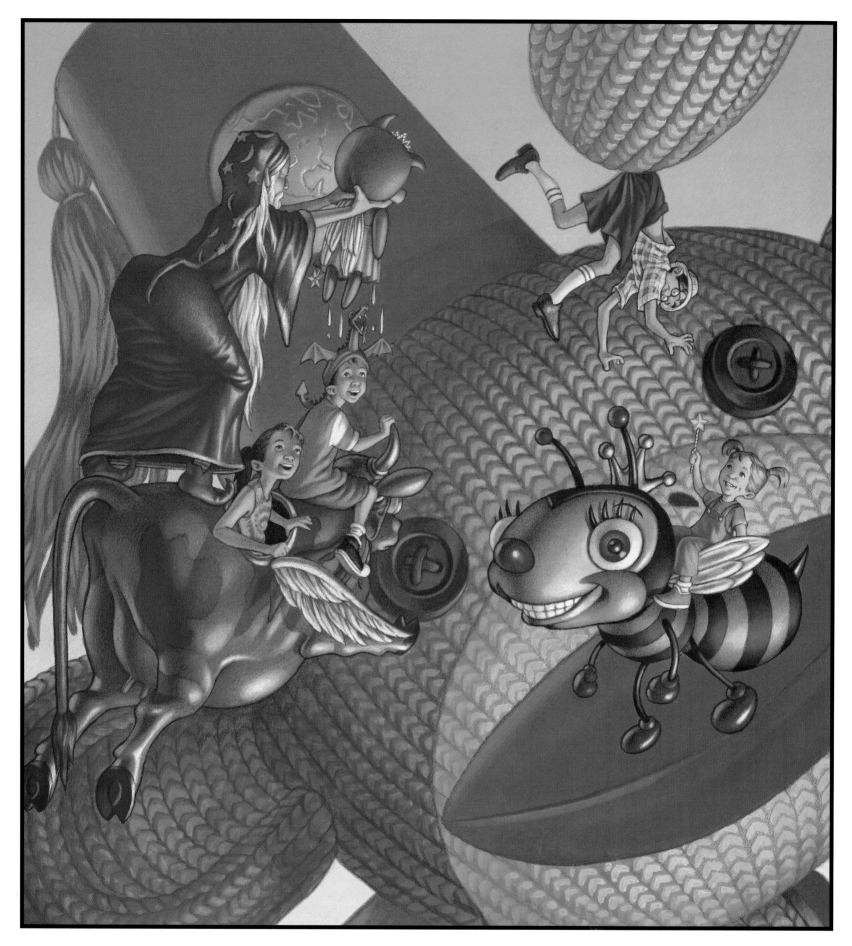

Daddy was in big, big trouble!

Pulling on the bumblebee's reins, the fearless toddler flew to the rescue. With one wave of her magic wand, Lulu made Oscar spit Daddy out and hand him over.

"Little girl," called the wizard, "wouldn't you like to trade my wand for Priscilla, the Fairy Piglet?"

Lulu's eyes lit up. She liked this idea.

But first she had something important to do. Lifting her hand high above her head, Lulu made one final wish and waved her wand over Adventure Planet.

Immediately, Oscar planted the Screamin' Dragon back in its place, then skipped back to his perch above the park's entrance gate.

The dinosaur opened his jagged mouth, and Mom and the cowboys carefully tiptoed out. One by one, all the other rides returned to normal too!

The wizard made the trade and bowed gratefully before Lulu. By the time he disappeared into the crowd, no one but Lulu remembered any of the day's magic.

Everyone was finally ready to go home. The toddler's eyes closed before the family even crossed the parking lot.

All of Lulu Winklewig's wishes had really come true. It had been a very big day for such a little girl.

As the car pulled out of the parking lot, Lulu cuddled up to Priscilla and dreamed about everything she'd wish for tomorrow.